Adapted by Brandon T. Snider
Based on the episode "Ghost in the Machine"
written by Len Uhley

LITTLE, BROWN & COMPANY
LB kids

Little, Brown and Company
Hachette Book Group
1290 Avenue of the Americas, New York, NY 10104
Visit us at lb-kids.com

First Edition: July 2017

LB kids is an imprint of Little, Brown and Company.
The LB kids name and logo are trademarks of Hachette Book Group, Inc.

The publisher is not responsible for websites (or their content) that are not owned by the publisher.

Library of Congress Control Number 2016949862

ISBNs: 978-0-316-31880-8 (pbk.), 978-0-316-31882-2 (ebook), 978-0-316-43628-1 (ebook), 978-0-316-43627-4 (ebook)

Printed in the United States of America

CW

10 9 8 7 6 5 4 3 2 1

Licensed By:

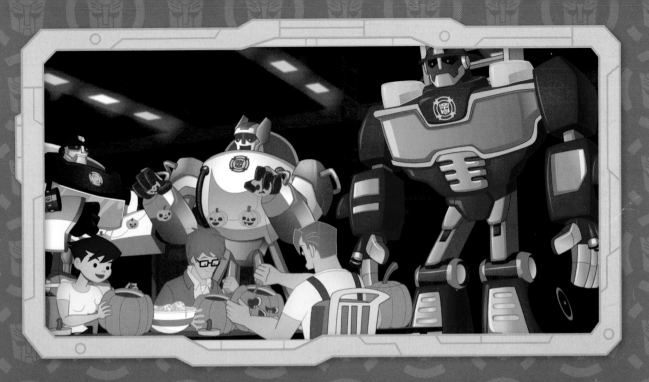

Every year, the people of Griffin Rock celebrate Halloween in warmer months. They call it "Earliween." The Rescue Bots decorate the firehouse while Kade, Dani, and Graham have fun carving jack-o'-lanterns.

Quickshadow's voice comes over the intercom. "Two humans are trying to steal me," she says.

"Rescue Bots, roll to the rescue!" Heatwave shouts. The Bots race out of the firehouse.

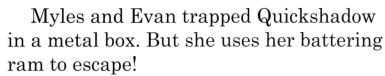

Myles and Evan trapped Quickshadow in a metal box. But she uses her battering ram to escape!

"It must be a self-driving car." says Myles. "We need to get our hands on that thing."

The Rescue Bots arrive, but the boys disappear before the Bots can catch them.

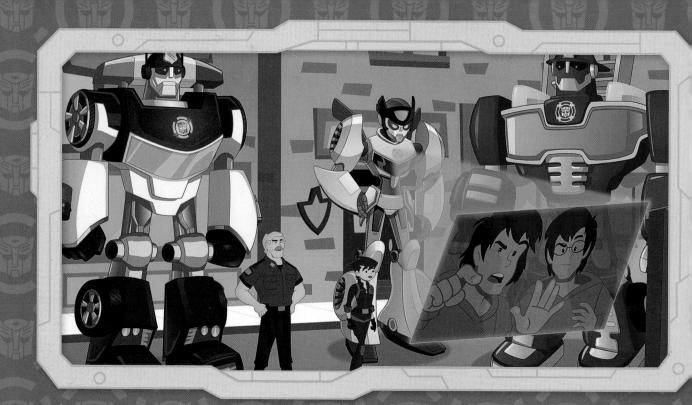

Quickshadow tells the Rescue Bots what happened. Everyone decides to keep an eye out for Myles and Evan while patrolling.

"I'm riding with her!" says Cody, hopping into Quickshadow.

In an underground tunnel, Evan and Myles plot their next move. When the Rescue Bots drive above them, Myles attaches a device to Quickshadow.

"That should do the trick!" Myles says.

Suddenly, Quickshadow can't control her steering.

"What's happening, Quickshadow?" Heatwave asks.

"I've lost control of my wheels, and I can't shut down my engine!" says Quickshadow. "Someone is controlling me remotely."

Cody hangs on tightly as they swerve dangerously through the streets.

"Whoever it is, they're sending us straight into the ocean!" exclaims Cody.

"Evan and Myles must have hacked into Quickshadow's system," Graham says.

From their van, Evan and Myles use a joystick to control Quickshadow. They make her zigzag across the road.

"We have to keep her from reaching the harbor," says Chief.

The Rescue Bots form a plan.
"We can block her," says Boulder.
"Get ready, everyone! Here she comes," says Heatwave.
"Remember that Cody is inside, so be careful!" reminds Chief.

"Watch out, Blades! They're controlling all my equipment," warns Quickshadow.

She launches a net toward Blades, but he avoids it.

Chase drives closer to Quickshadow. She sprays oil all over the street. Chase spins out of control!

Boulder stacks dumpsters and pipes, making a roadblock. "This should stop her," he says.

Quickshadow fires her rocket boosters and soars over the big pile of junk.

Next it is Kade and Heatwave's turn to try to stop Quickshadow.

Kade strings one of Heatwave's fire hoses across an intersection.

"She won't get past this," says Heatwave.

Quickshadow uses a magnetic claw to grab ahold of a lamppost. She changes course and speeds around them, toward the dock.

Quickshadow drives into the ocean! Heatwave changes into boat mode and takes off after her. Blades lowers his winch, picks up Boulder, and heads out to sea.

Underwater, Quickshadow realizes the device is attached to her undercarriage. She has an idea.

"Blades, might I trouble you for a lift?" she asks.

Blades lowers Boulder into the ocean. He grabs Quickshadow's bumper and lifts her out of the water. Chief Burns and Kade pull Cody to safety.

Boulder lets go of Quickshadow. As she falls, she changes into Bot mode and finds the control device near her arm. She lands on the rocks, removing the device.

"A Cybertronian will not be controlled—on this or any other planet," says Quickshadow.

In their van, Myles and Evan watch the Rescue Bots in secret and are stunned by what they see and hear.

"That isn't a car or a robot. They're aliens!" says Myles to Evan. "We're going to tell everyone."

Back at the firehouse, the Rescue Bots are ready for the Earliween festivities.

"Now we can trick-or-treat and bob for apples!" says Blades.

A jack-o'-lantern sits on the ground nearby. Its eyes begin to glow, and a hologram of Myles and Evan appears before the team.

"Hello, Rescue Bots. We know you're aliens," Myles says. "Hand over Little Miss Spy Car or we'll tell the whole world. We've got it all on video. This pumpkin will self-destruct in one second."

The jack-o'-lantern explodes, covering everyone in goo.

"So I guess we're not trick-or-treating?" asks Blades, disappointed.

"I've got an idea!" Boulder says. "We'll make people think we're *make-believe* aliens."

"Yeah! If Myles and Evan can make a video, so can we!" Cody says.

The Rescue Bots gather what they need. Graham sets up his camera equipment, and Kade starts filming.

"Action!" Cody shouts.

Later, Quickshadow turns herself over to Myles and Evan. "I'm here to surrender," she says, opening her doors. The two brothers gleefully jump inside.

CA-CHUNK! The safety harnesses lock them into their seats.

"Sorry, lads, but this treat just turned into a trick," Quickshadow says.

"Too late!" says Myles. "Evan already uploaded *Aliens Are Real* to the Internet. Now, everyone knows about you and your alien buddies."

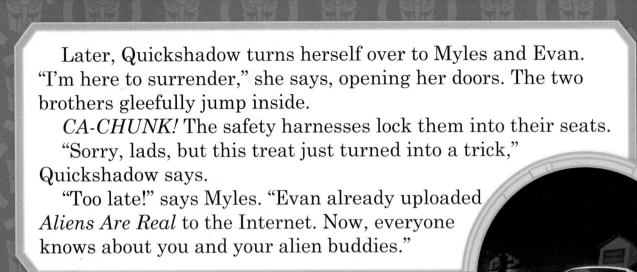

"It's a good thing we created a sequel," Quickshadow says.

Her dashboard lights up as a video shows the Rescue Bots pretending to attack Griffin Rock.

"That is so fake! No one will ever believe it," says Myles.

"You're right. And that means they won't believe your video, either," Quickshadow says.

"Happy Earliween!" everyone cheers as the video ends.

"But you *are* aliens!" Myles grumps as Quickshadow takes him and Evan to jail.

"Always remember—just because something is on the Internet, that doesn't mean it's real," Cody says.

"I couldn't agree more!" says Blades. "Now can we go trick-or-treating?!"